WITHDRAWN

World of Reading

LEVEL 1

THIS IS IRON MAN

By Thomas Macri

Illustrated by Craig Rousseau *and* Hi-Fi Design

Based on the Marvel comic book series The Invincible Iron Man

ABDO
Spotlight

New York

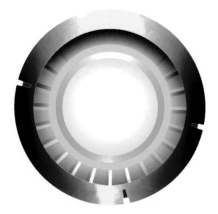

WWW.ABDOPUBLISHING.COM

Reinforced library bound edition published in 2015 by Spotlight, a division of ABDO
PO Box 398166, Minneapolis, Minnesota 55439. Spotlight produces high-quality
reinforced library bound editions for schools and libraries. Published by Marvel Press,
an imprint of Disney Book Group.

Printed in the United States of America, North Mankato, Minnesota.
052014
072014

TM & © 2012 Marvel & Subs.

Published by Marvel Press, an imprint of Disney Book Group. No part of this book may
be reproduced or transmitted in any form or by any means, electronic or mechanical,
including photocopying, recording, or by any information storage and retrieval system,
without written permission from the publisher. For information address Marvel Press,
114 5th Avenue, New York, New York 10011-5690.

LIBRARY OF CONGRESS CATALOGING-IN-PUBLICATION DATA

This title was previously cataloged with the following information:

Macri, Thomas.
This is Ironman / by Thomas Macri ; illustrated by Craig Rousseau and Hi-Fi Design.
  p. cm. -- (World of reading. Level 1)
Summary: Introduces the superhero Iron Man, explaining what makes him special.
1. Iron Man (Fictitious characters)--Juvenile fiction. 2. Superheroes--Juvenile fiction. I.
Rousseau, Craig, ill. II. Hi-Fi Colour Design, ill. III. Title. IV. Series.
PZ7.M24731Th 2012
[Fic]--dc23

2012289468

978-1-61479-254-3 (Reinforced Library Bound Edition)

Spotlight
A Division of ABDO
www.abdopublishing.com

This is Tony.

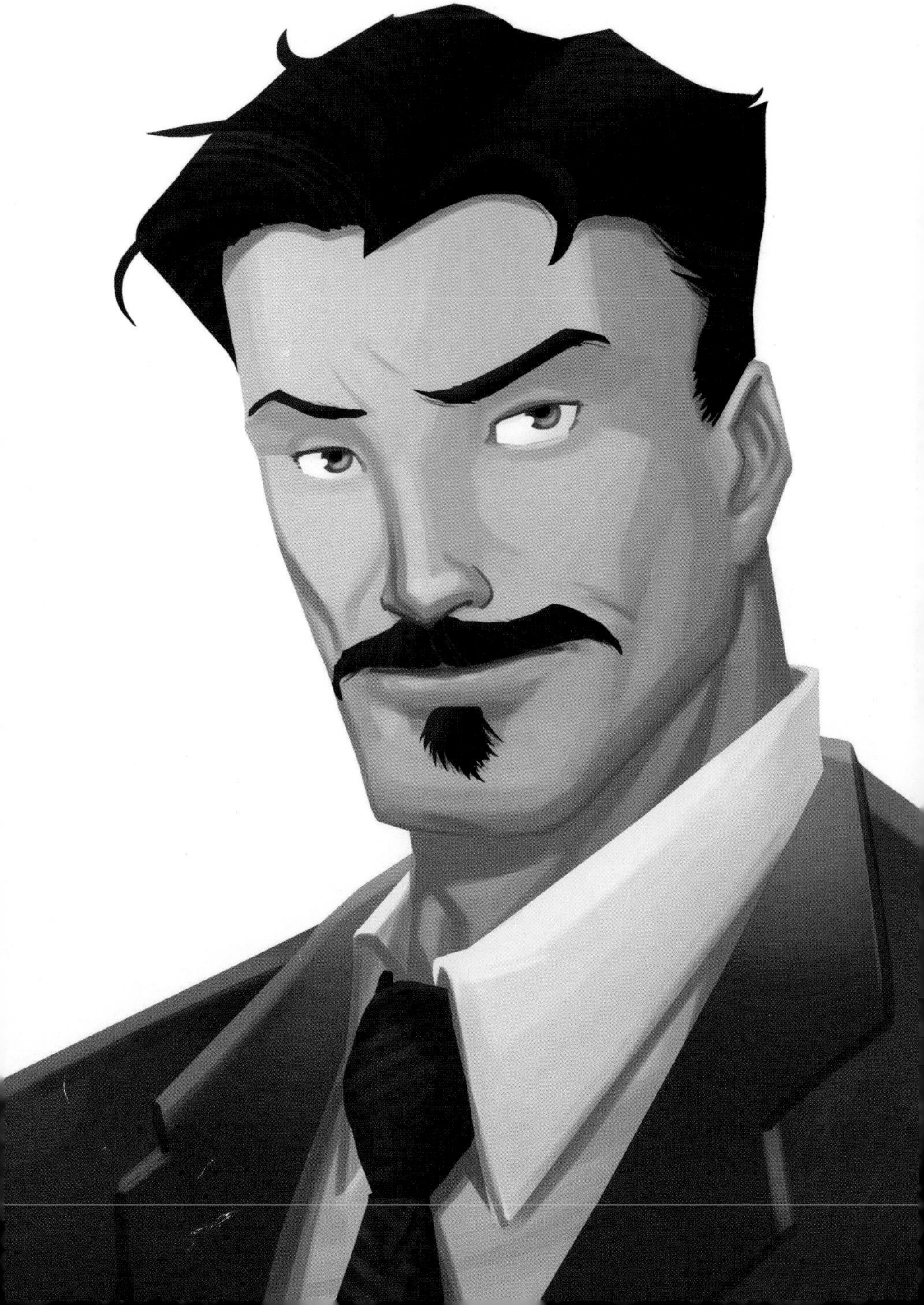

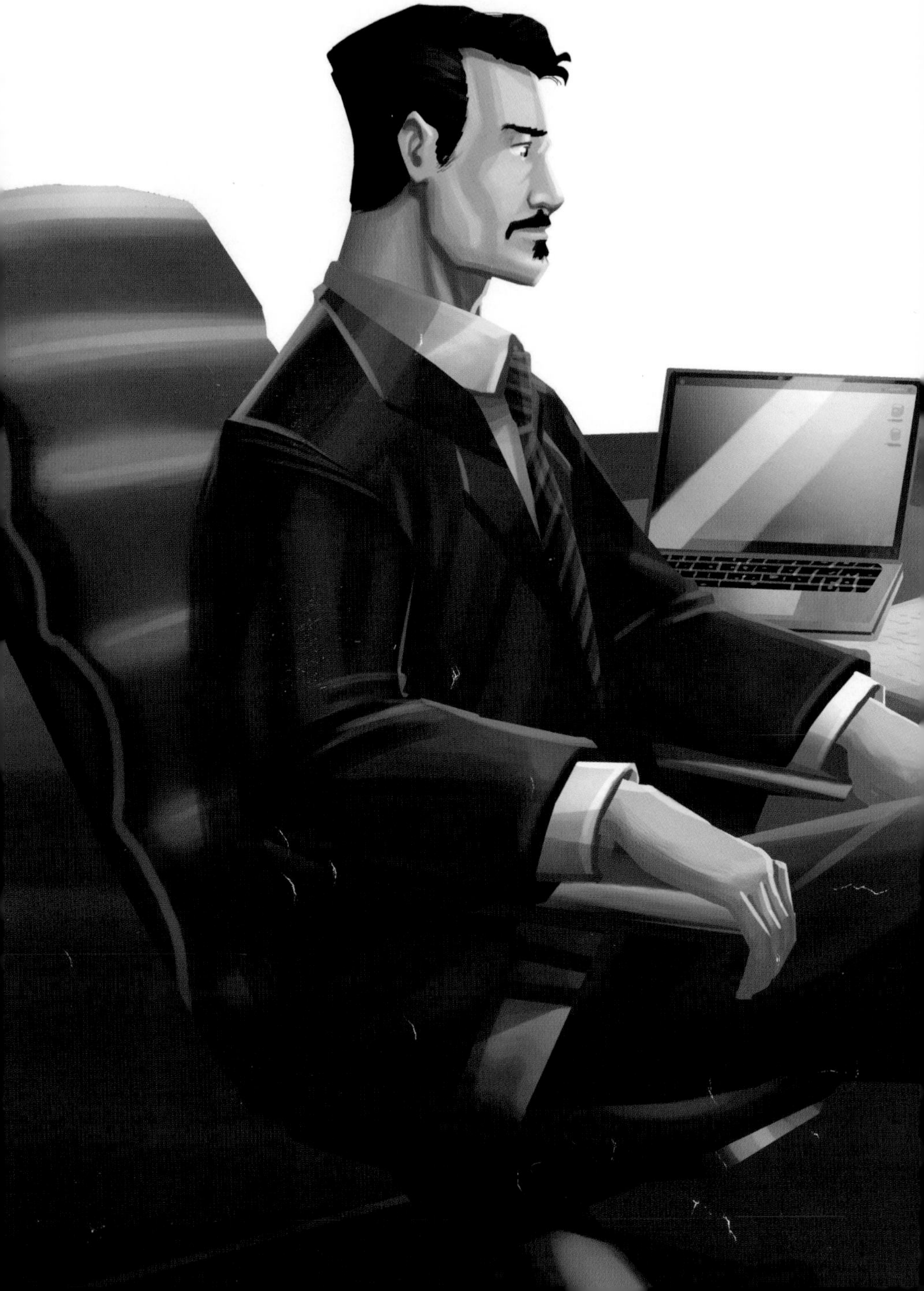

He owns a company.
It is called Stark.
Stark is also his
last name.

Tony is rich.

He has a beach house.

He has a house in
the city.

He has a boat that is big
as a house.
He has a house as big as
an island.

Tony has good friends.
He works with his friend
Pepper Potts.

Tony has a friend named
James Rhodes.
Tony calls him Rhodey.
Rhodey works for the army.

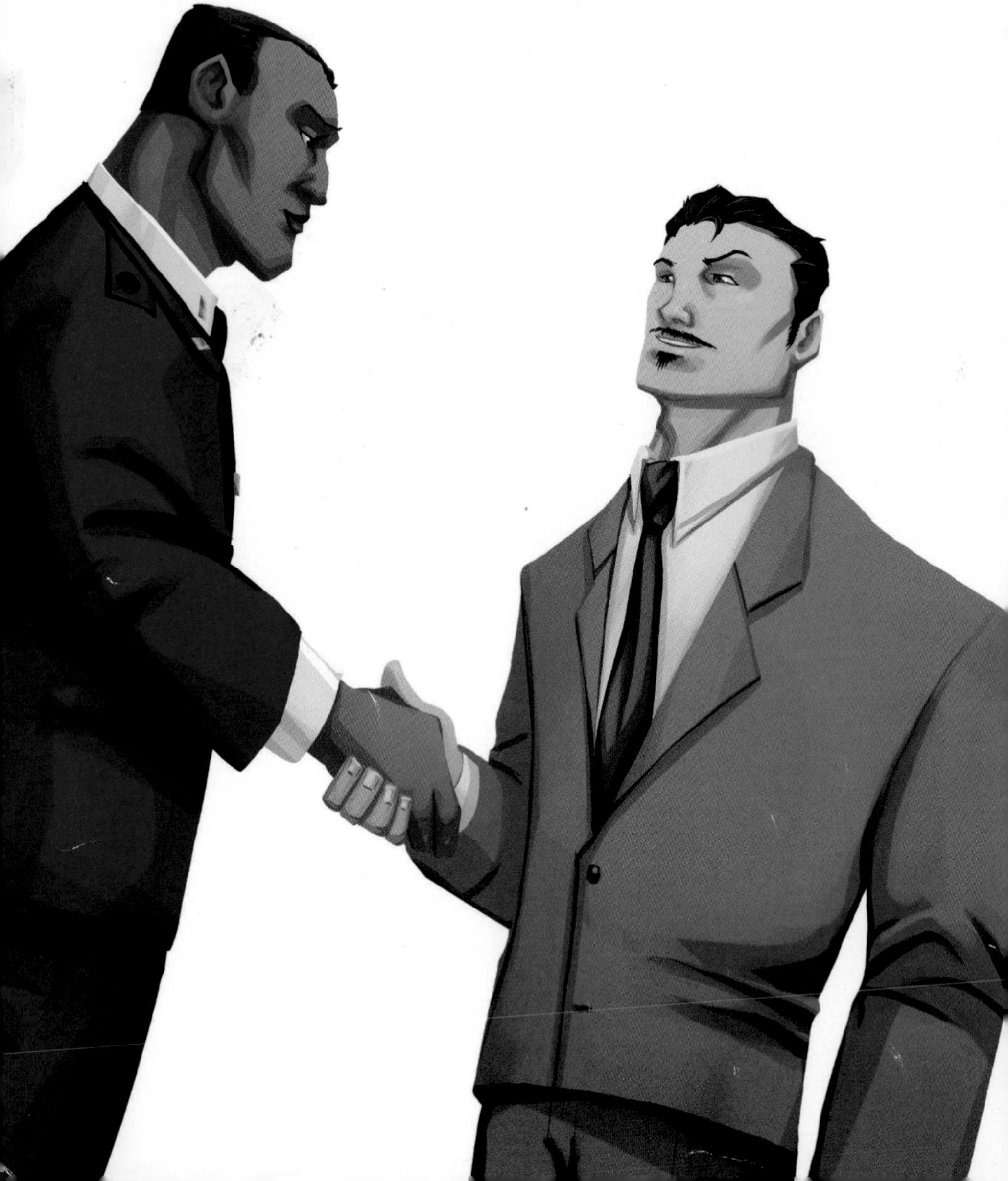

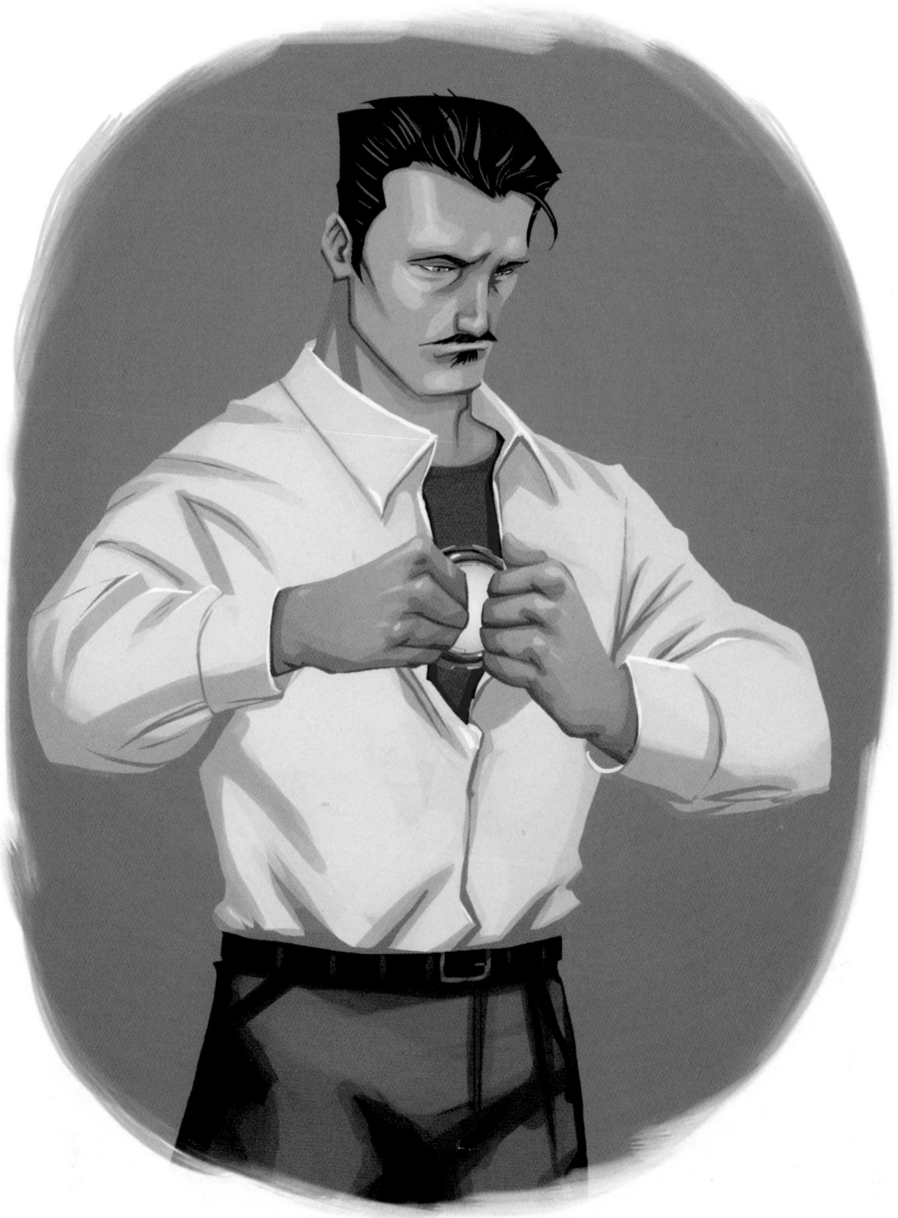

Tony has a secret.

Tony wears a disk.
It keeps him alive.

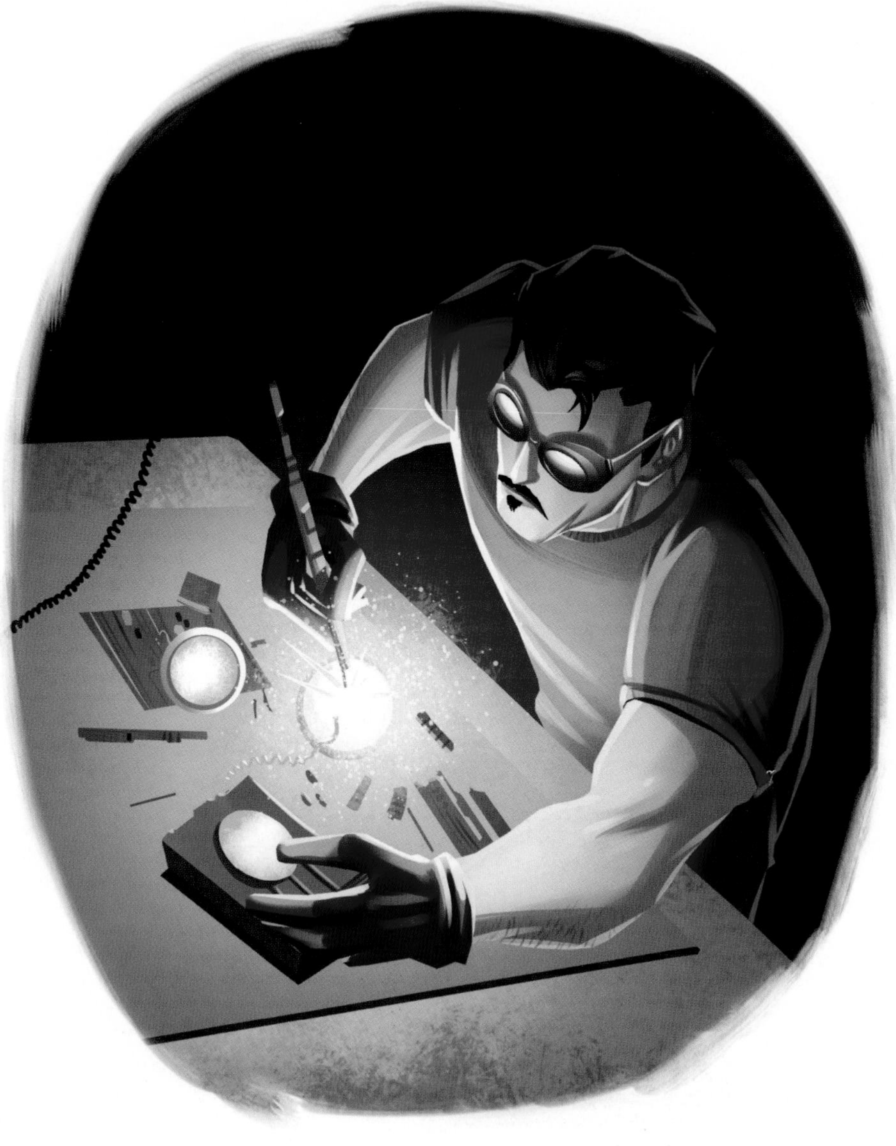

He made the disk.

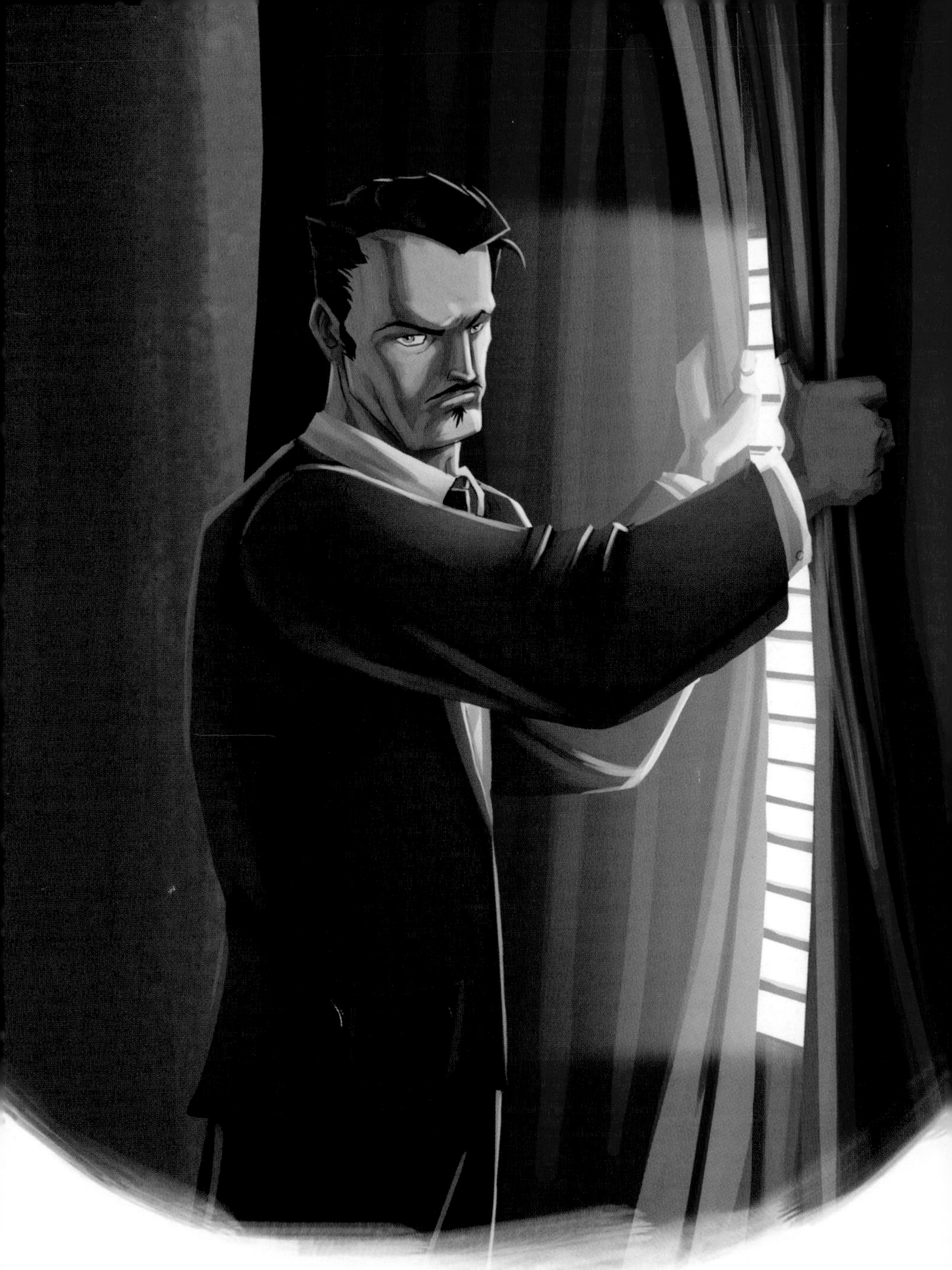

But that is not all.

Tony has a bigger secret.
He keeps it in his case.

He keeps a suit with him.

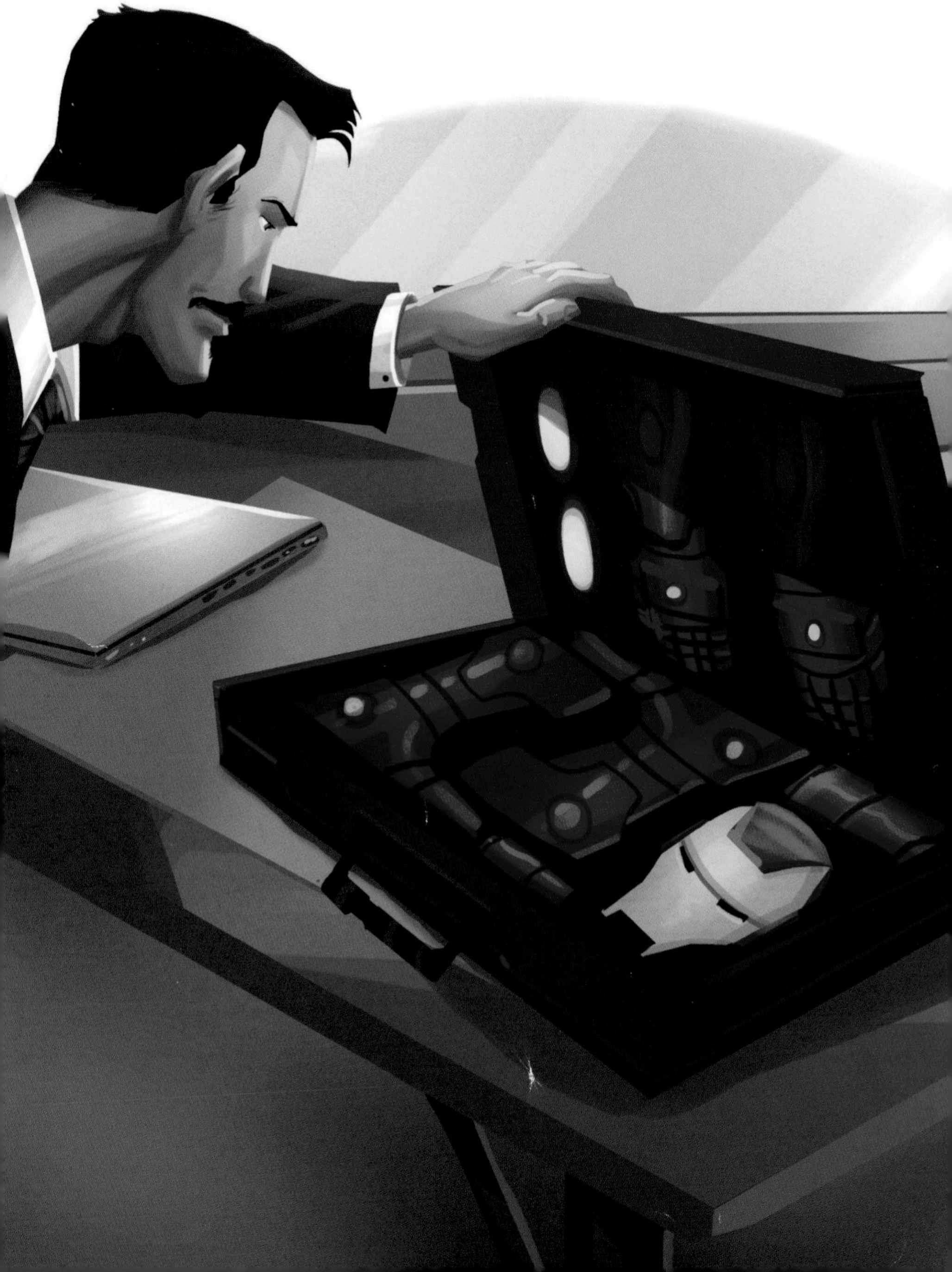

He puts on the suit.

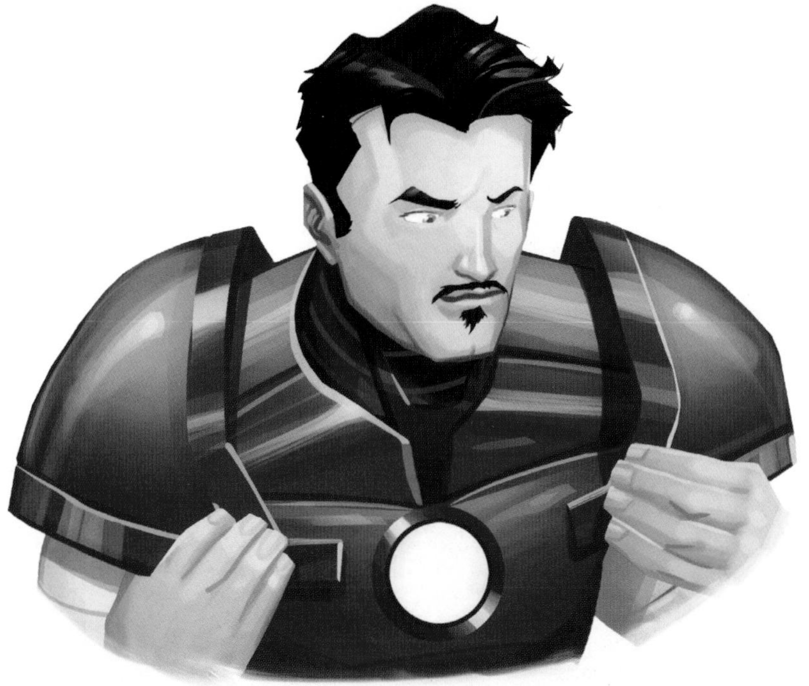

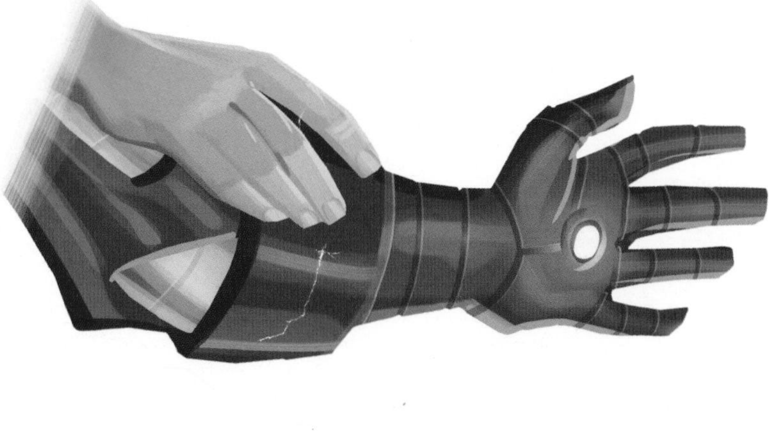

This is Tony's big secret.
He is a Super Hero!

Tony puts on his helmet.
He has a secret name.
He calls himself
Iron Man.

This is Iron Man.

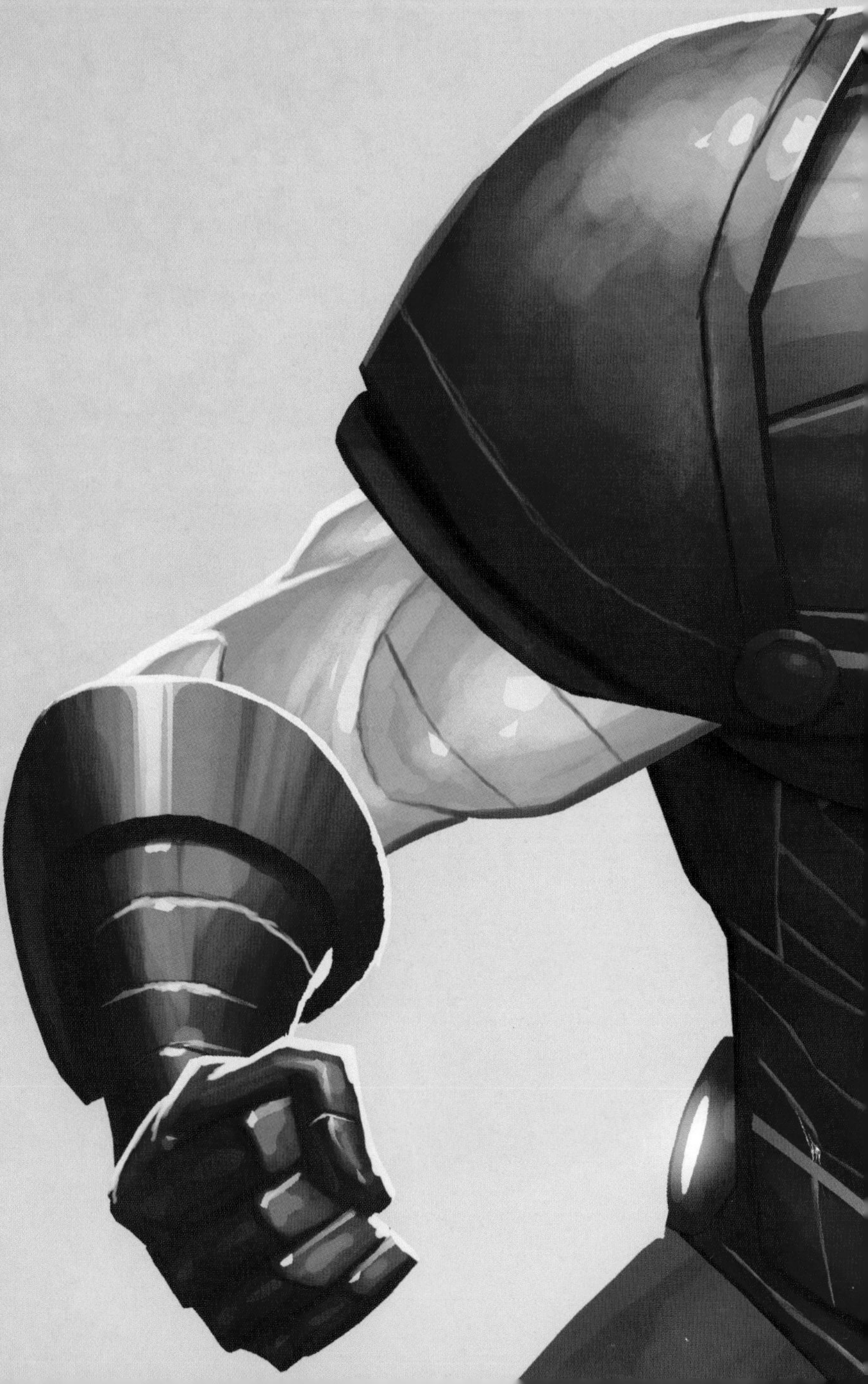

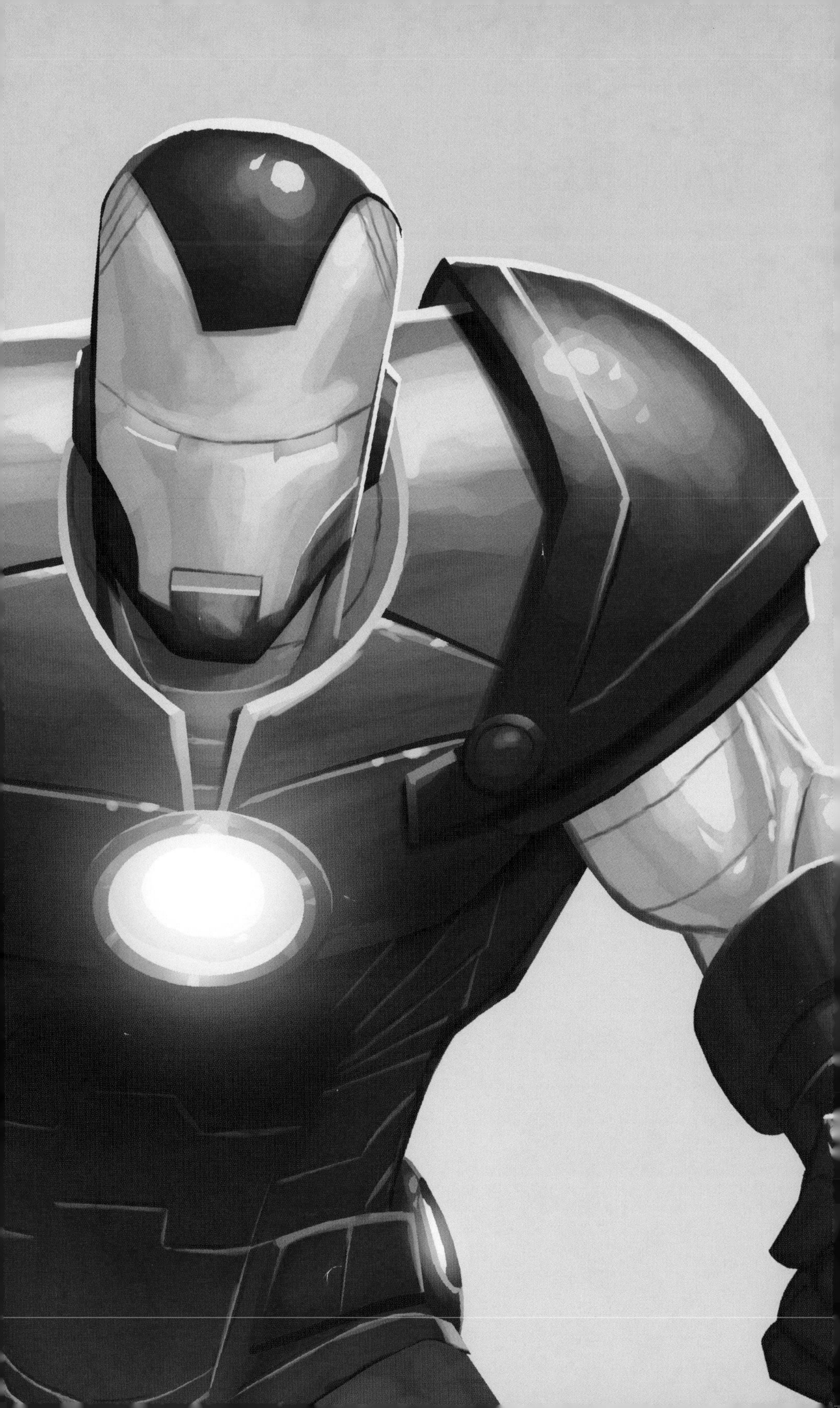

Iron Man can fly.

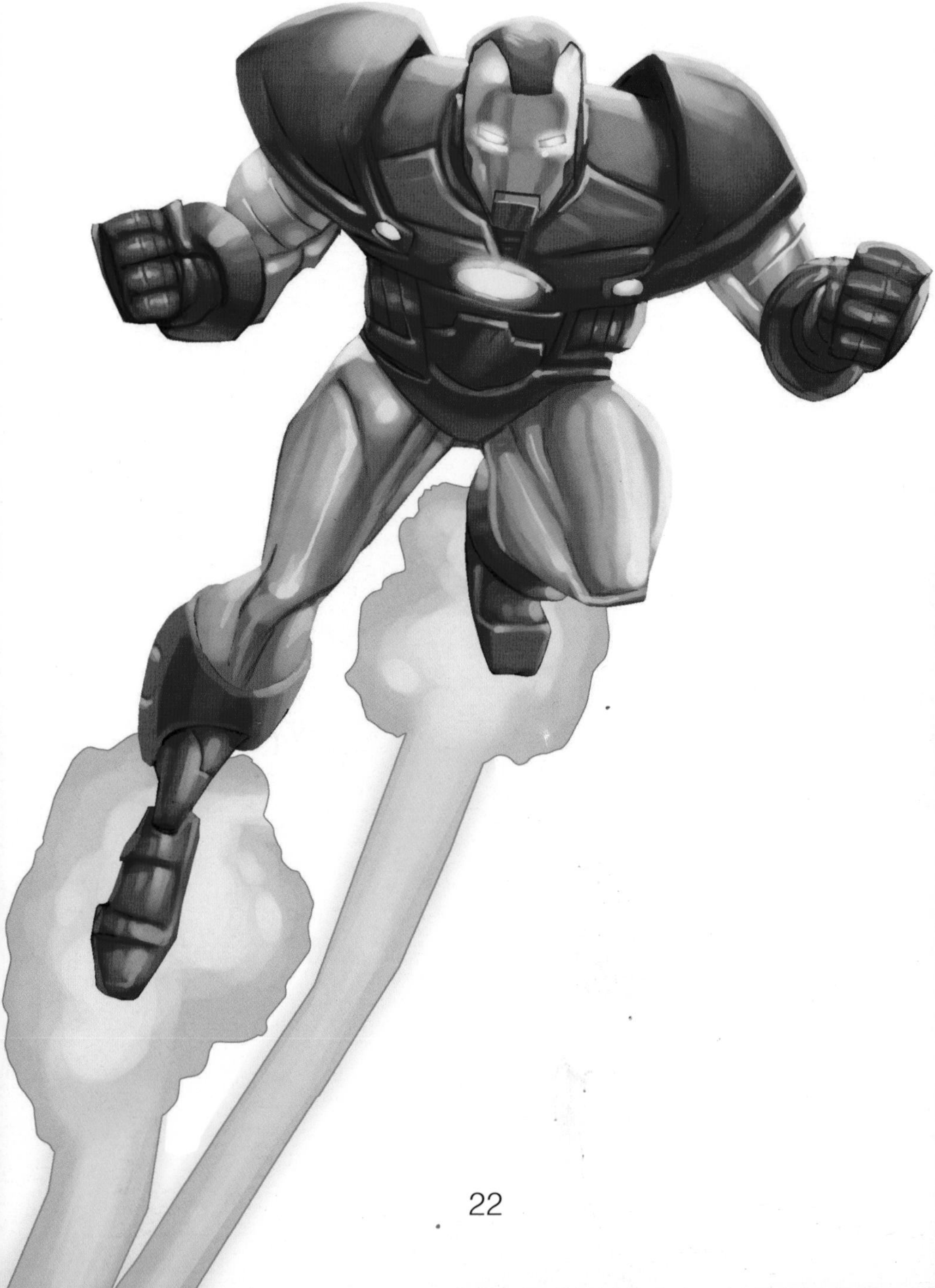

He can shoot
repulsor blasts.

Iron Man shoots
his blasts.
They stop bad guys.

Tony's suit makes
him strong.

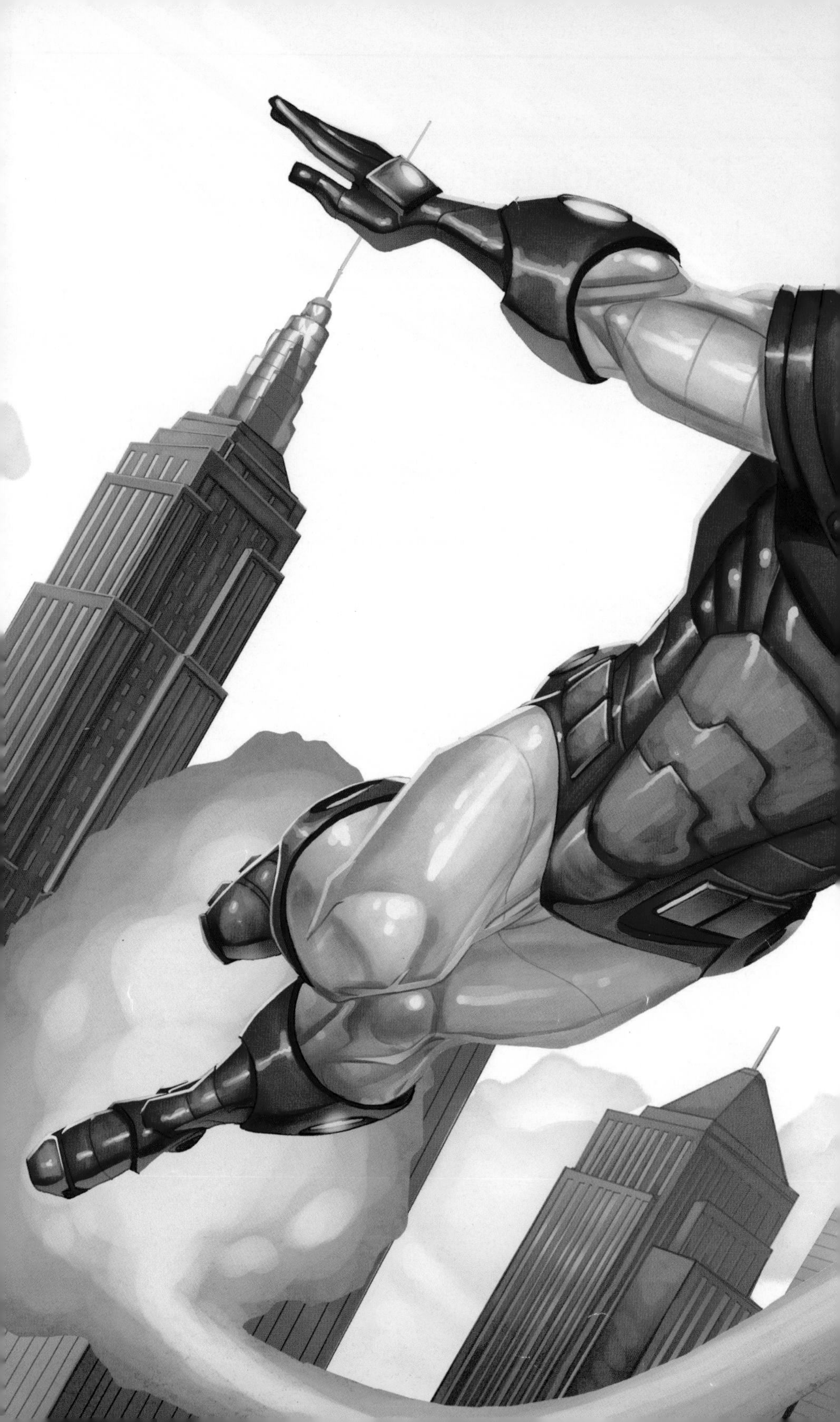

It makes him
a Super Hero.

Tony works to make his
suit better.

He tests new things.

He tries new suits.

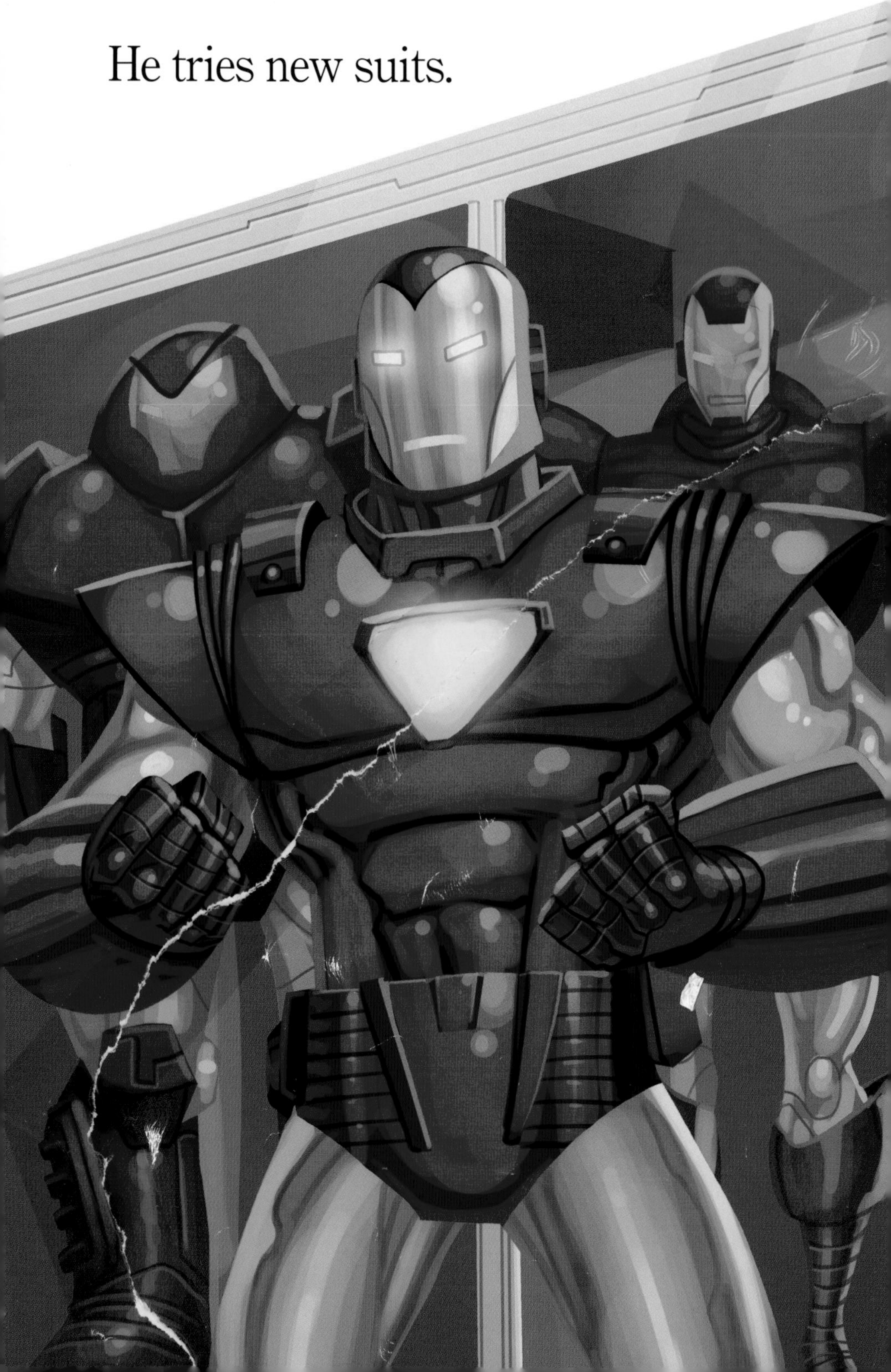

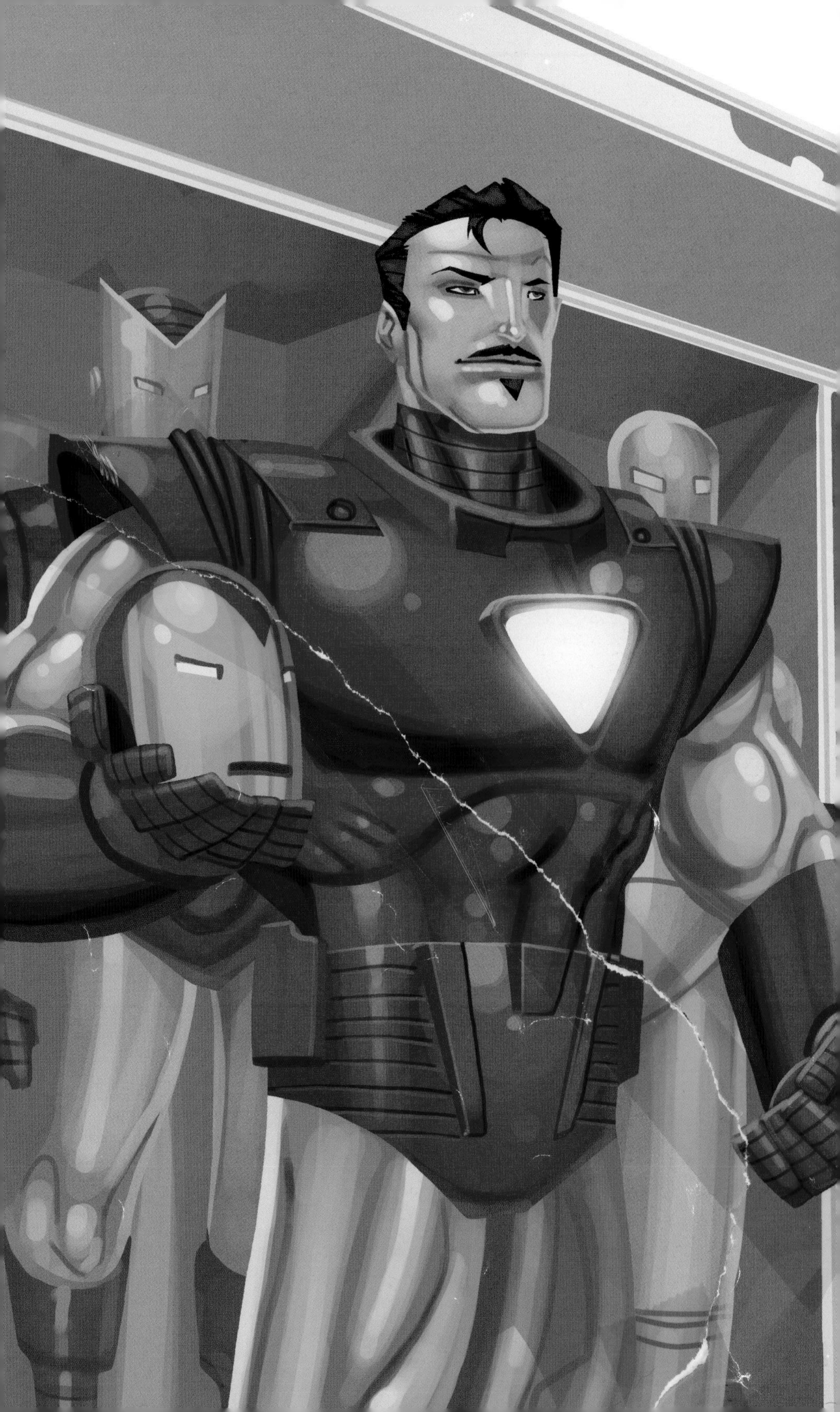

The man inside is
the same.
He is Tony.

He is Iron Man.

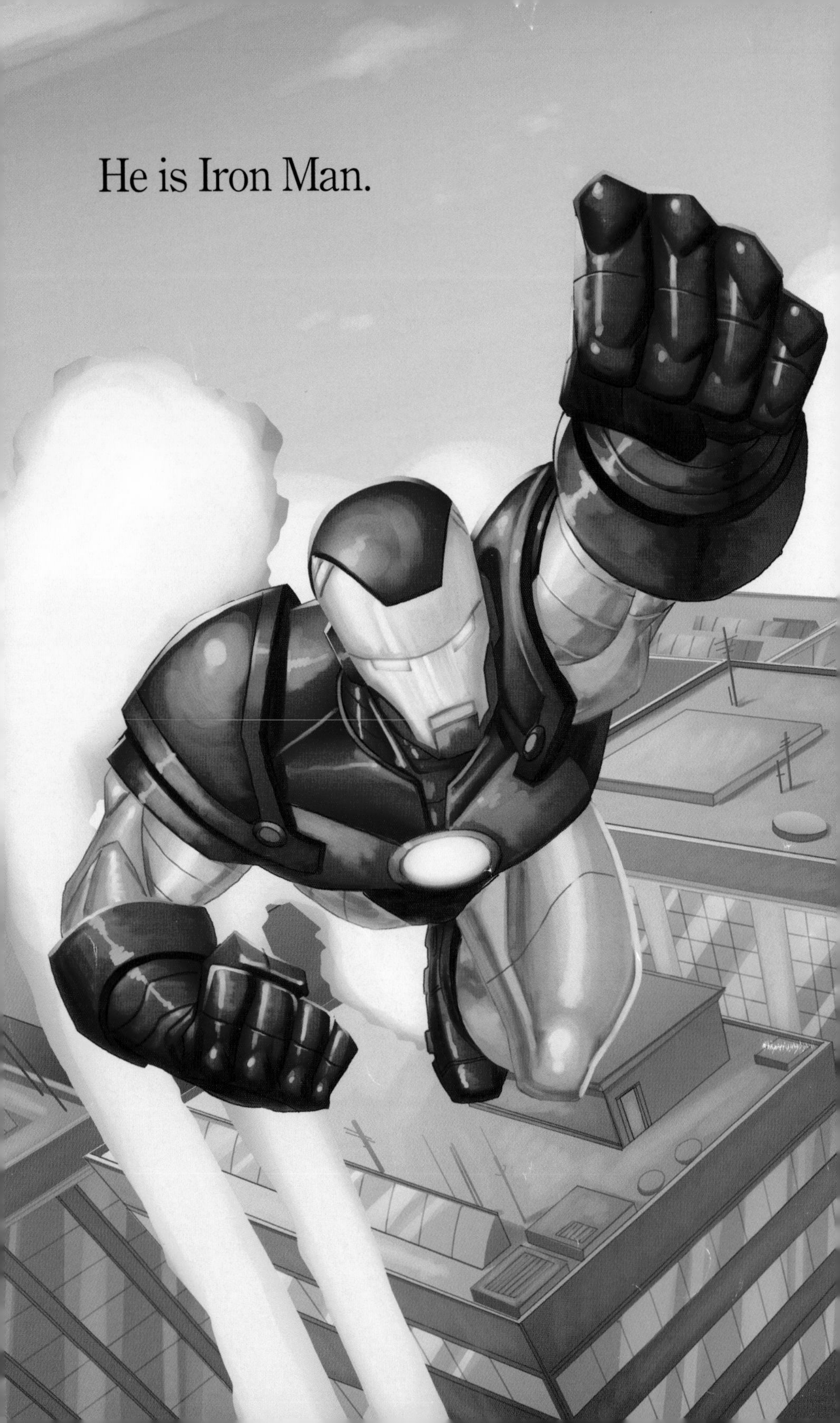

CONTRA COSTA COUNTY LIBRARY

31901064931381